The 10

Prof. P.R. Mukund is an electronics engineer who has spent 36 years in academia and six years in industry. He is a globally acclaimed expert in the field of analog and radio frequency integrated circuit design and has led many research projects for both the government and the semiconductor industry. He has published extensively in international journals and participated in conferences worldwide.

Prof. Mukund is also a student and teacher of Vedic science and spirituality, and guides hundreds of people in every aspect of life. In 2006, he started Tara Prakashana (taraprakashana.org), a non-profit trust that has saved thousands of palm-leaf manuscripts through the use of modern technology. His work has been reported in major news outlets such as BBC, MSNBC, CNN, *The Times of India* and other leading global media outlets.

Follow him on:
LinkedIn: linkedin.com/in/p-r-mukund-4231962b
Twitter: twitter.com/ProfPRMukund
YouTube: youtube.com/c/ProfPRMukund

The 10 Gunas (MINDSETS)
for **JIVA** (YOU), **JIVAN** (LIFE)
and **MOKSHA** (FULFILMENT)

Prof. P.R. Mukund

RUPA

Published by
Rupa Publications India Pvt. Ltd 2022
7/16, Ansari Road, Daryaganj
New Delhi 110002

Sales centres:
Allahabad Bengaluru Chennai
Hyderabad Jaipur Kathmandu
Kolkata Mumbai

ISBN: 978-93-5520-561-2

First impression 2022

10 9 8 7 6 5 4 3 2 1

The moral right of the author has been asserted.

Printed in India

CONTENTS

INTRODUCTION

A few years ago, I was invited to speak at a conference on the theme of 'Science and Spirituality'. My talk was on 'Veda and Electronics', and the organizers expected an audience of around a hundred people. However, something unexpected happened just before my talk—hundreds of students from local engineering colleges turned up, so the organizers had to delay my talk and move it to a much bigger hall. I've had similar experiences when I gave talks on similar topics at Indian Institute of Technology campuses, Amity University, Jawaharlal Nehru University, People's Education Society University and numerous other venues in India.

In my chosen field of electrical engineering, I have given numerous technical talks the world over, but they never reach the level of enthusiasm that I see for my talks connecting 'science' and 'spirituality'.

Perhaps it is because it connects material science with energy science. If material science explains how things work, spiritual science explains why things work. These two domains are often treated as orthogonal viewpoints that cannot coexist. It is often thought that any science related to energy cannot pass the rigid test of material science, and as such, it cannot be scientific at all. The fact is that any scientific principle, material or otherwise, starts off as a hypothesis. A controlled experiment is designed to test its validity. After conducting the experiment repeatedly for many types of inputs, the hypothesis is either accepted as a scientific fact or discarded as baseless. This changes, over time, as new hypotheses are presented and science evolves. This very same process can be applied to energy-related hypotheses as well.

In the Vedic world, such experimental validation has been conducted for thousands of years, and the resultant scientific theories have been upheld over a long period of time. As such, the two sides of the universe, matter and energy, both lend themselves to the same scrutiny and are equally valid. The connection between the two is what is, somewhat erroneously, called science and spirituality. The connections are not only fascinating but can also solve problems that neither can do individually. The theories presented in this book are an amalgamation of this bridge between the material and the spiritual.

My Background

I was born and raised in India, one of many children in a middle-class family. It was a carefree childhood, and I did not even go to school until I was six years old. My family lived outside the city limits where the only water source was a well and the only way to get to the house was a path cleared by frequent usage. My favourite pastime was sitting high up the branches of a guava tree and doing literally nothing. Nobody asked me to dream of success. Come to think of it, I do not recall anyone telling me to do anything. There was no pressure to perform, no commitment to competition and definitely no exposure to much of the world.

When I was four or five years old, I got my first haircut. When I was six years old, I was sent to school. That was my first exposure to the world. It was odd that based on only a few questions, the school decided that I could skip the first standard and go straight to the second standard. In school, I met a couple of boys and started playing on the very first day. After 63 years, we are still good friends and meet as often as we can.

School was a bit of an eye-opener. For the first time, I saw the parents of some of my friends come to school to talk to teachers about their children. I wondered why my parents never came to school. My friends would talk about places they had visited on holidays. I had never gone anywhere on a vacation. Some of them would talk about going to eat at restaurants or watching movies at movie theaters. I never had an opportunity to do either.

There were two scary experiences in school when I was about eight or nine years old. They both taught me different lessons. I don't recall the exact sequence. But one day, the school decided to change the seating system in the classroom. There were about 50 students, somewhat equal number of boys and girls. There was no assigned seating. All the boys sat on one side, and the girls sat on the other side. This worked well for us because we could sit with our friends and have a good time. But the teachers felt that the boys were being a little too boisterous. So, they came up with a new seating plan, with boys and girls sitting next to each other. Like any self-respecting eight-year-old boy, I hated this arrangement. So, I decided to show my displeasure by hitting the girl next to me with my metal lunch box. Unfortunately, the sharp edge of the box caused a nick in the girl's ankle, and a drop of blood came out. She was furious and told me that they had a servant at home who would 'take care of me' the next day. To my horror, the servant did show up the next day at lunchtime and was looking for me. I got terribly scared and climbed a tree, and I stayed there until I was sure that the servant was gone. This incident taught me a very important lesson: *never lash out at others when you are unhappy with a situation. This will only make matters worse and does little to help the situation.*

The second incident was more liberating, even though I was scared at the time it happened. One day, at lunchtime in school, my friend noticed that I had not brought lunch. He was from a rich family and always had money. He offered to take me to a restaurant and buy me lunch. At home, we had been raised with strict rules of not eating outside food, but I decided to take up my friend's offer. The forbidden food was tasty and exciting, with no bad outcomes. I learnt something from this experience as well: *without taking risks, one will always live within the confines of safety and never experience the excitement of freedom.*

A few years went by, and the seventh-standard exam (graduating from middle school to high school) was a district-level public examination. To my pleasant surprise, I passed with a first-class and was invited to an award ceremony the following year. It happened to be the fiftieth anniversary of the school's founding, and the noted diplomat and politician Vijaya Lakshmi Pandit was the chief guest who would give away the awards. I reached the school ahead of time and noticed that other students were accompanied by their parents, many of whom had cameras to capture the memorable moment. I was alone and decided that some quick thinking was needed to avoid being left behind. I noticed that the press was in full attendance for the event. I approached the official photographer of the leading English newspaper *Deccan Herald*. I spoke to him respectfully and explained that I was alone and needed his help. I told him that if he took my picture receiving the award and gave me a copy, I would somehow come up with some money to pay for it. The gentleman was amused and agreed to give me a photograph at no cost. I realized a lack of resources need not limit one from reaching for something beyond one's reach. People admire grit and determination, and often come to the rescue of the helpless.

High school was fairly uneventful. The next decision point came when I finished my pre-university course. To my pleasant surprise, I got admission by merit to both BSc (Hons.) in physics and engineering. I was confused. I did not know which subject to choose. Suddenly, I had a eureka moment. I realized that up until that point,

I had never asked my father for advice. Neither had he offered any, on any topic. So, one evening, I decided to ask his opinion. He was relaxing in the open air, reading a newspaper. I went and stood at a distance. He finished what he was reading, looked up and asked what I wanted. I blurted out my dilemma and asked him what he would advise me to do. He listened and looked into space. I eagerly awaited his words of wisdom. After staring at nothing for a few seconds, he looked at me and said, 'I tell you what you should do. Study whichever you like better,' and went back to his newspaper. That was the only advice I ever got from my father.

I had read a book by Prof. Carl Sagan, the famous American astronomer. I was always fascinated by the starlit skies of Bangalore (now Bengaluru) in the 1950s. Just looking at the sky was a spiritual experience. So, I joined the BSc (Hons.) course in physics at the age of 16. My cohorts of less than two dozen were a studious group. But I was bored. I found the classes very insipid. And the teenage mind was getting more attracted to adventure. The perfect outlet for adventure came in the form of the National Cadet Corps (NCC).

I had been active in the naval wing of the NCC from my high-school days. The white uniform was fascinating. I had gone to an annual camp in Mangalore for 10 days when I was in high school. The memories of the Arabian Sea and ships far on the horizon beckoned me. I decided to put my heart and soul into NCC training in college. My uniform was always the whitest, best-starched and ironed. I was even selected to participate in the Republic Day parade in Delhi. Marching on the Rajpath in front of the president of India was a proud moment. I attended camps in Cochin, Visakhapatnam, Kashmir and so on. I became a senior cadet captain and was adjudged the 'Best Cadet' at the Karnataka state-level camp. It seemed like my destiny was chosen. And so, I ignored my studies. I barely scraped through my final-year exams.

The time had come to start my adventure in the Indian Navy. I waited for the announcement for applications. The awaited advertisement finally came. I applied for a commission in the Naval Aviation branch of the Indian Navy. I was selected for a multi-day interview at the Service Selection

Board (SSB) campus in Mysore. On the very first day, we had to appear for a pilot aptitude test. Half of the more than 50 candidates could not pass and were sent home. I was told that I had scored the highest-recorded score at that SSB. I was elated. At the end of another three days of various activities and interviews, I was one of the two candidates selected. We were asked to report to the Institute of Aviation Medicine in Bangalore. At the end of the second day there, I was rejected on medical grounds. The reason was a condition called chorioretinitis, essentially a small dot on the retina in my right eye. This little tiny dot brought down years of hard work, dreams, adventure and what appeared to be a successful future. At the young age of 21, it seemed like I was done.

But nothing is over until it is really over. Yes, I had no apparent career path, no proper education, no connections and no financial backing. But on the flip side, I was young, energetic, optimistic and willing to work hard. So, I decided to go to Germany to study and work. But around that time, one of my sisters got married to a person settled in the United States (US). Upon his advice and initial help, I ended up in Nashville, a pleasant southern city in the country.

It was impossible to go to a regular university, both because of cost and lack of academic background. So, I was enrolled in a small technical institute to get an associate degree that would enable me to work as an electronic technician. Soon, I found that I could not work outside the small campus due to visa regulations. The only job I could get was that of a janitor. I studied during the day and worked full-time as a janitor from four in the evening till midnight.

Sweeping floors, cleaning toilets and removing trash from offices were some of my responsibilities. It was a new life and a new experience. The hard-working but uneducated people I worked with were some of the nicest people I have come across in my life.

I went from being a janitor to a technician. From there, while working to support myself, I got a bachelor's and master's degree in electrical engineering. I worked as an R&D (research and development) engineer for five years and went back to get a PhD. For more than three decades,

I have been on the faculty of engineering in a major university in the US. I have brought in millions of dollars in research funding, educated many engineers, including many PhD-level students. I have chaired many international conferences, have been invited to give talks in many countries and have had a very successful career.

The success was not just professional. Today, I have a beautiful family, with children and grandchildren who are very close to me. Moreover, I have been able to pass on our culture to two generations.

I also have a wonderful spiritual life. An amazing Vedic scholar, Dr Bannanje Govindacharya, accepted me as his disciple. I learnt so much about Vedic science and had so many surreal experiences. A shishya searches for a guru, but it is actually the guru who finds the shishya. It took me a while to truly understand the guru–shishya relationship. It is like a transformer in a charger that brings down the voltage to a manageable level and charges a device. The guru brings down infinite knowledge to our level and pours it into us like a funnel. Without such a relationship, it is very difficult to access the infinite amount of knowledge and energy that is present in the universe.

Today, I head a non-profit trust that has saved thousands of ancient manuscripts. Many successful professionals seek spiritual guidance from me. I have given talks in leading universities and corporations in India. I have been able to absolve the misconceptions in the minds of thousands of youngsters about the Vedic way of life. I tell them about the 10 gunas (mindsets). I tell them how the 10 guiding principles—*jnana, bhakti, vairagya, pragnya, medha shakti, dhriti, stithi, yoga, prana shakti* and *bala*—changed my life, and how it can transform theirs.

Jnana is knowledge that transforms into wisdom with experience. That leads to respect, devotion and passion—collectively, this is bhakti. When we are facing something big, smaller things fade into insignificance—reaching that state of detached attachment is vairagya. Pragnya is the awareness of truth in our surroundings that go beyond normal perception. It is essential to recall lessons learnt, in real time, to make good decisions in the present— the ability to do that is medha shakti. A sincere effort to grow these five traits will result in the other five traits that are essential for success in life. Dhriti is having confidence in ourselves and the universe in its ultimate righteousness. That would give us conviction and strength in our values and beliefs, which is stithi. A balanced life is yoga, which gives us the prana shakti or the energy to succeed. Lastly, we have bala or strength in physical, mental and spiritual layers.

This universe is full of both living and non-living things. These are called *jiva* and *jada*, respectively. No two pieces of matter, even at the atomic level, are exactly alike. Then there are living things. There are millions of fascinating species. No two species are alike, and even within a given species, no two living things are exactly alike. Only humans are blessed with the unique ability to differentiate between right and wrong, good and bad. While other species may live and enjoy their given bodies, man alone seeks fulfilment. How exactly does one achieve fulfilment? To answer this question, if we can look at the number system, we find a good analogy. There are three divisions. There is zero, infinity and finite numbers. Zero and infinity have unique properties. All other numbers, no matter how small or large, have to follow the rules of arithmetic. No two numbers are equal, but all are equally important in the number system. Any number, big or small, can tend towards infinity when divided by zero.

Similarly, we are all unique and different. No two of us are exactly equal or alike. But the awareness of our nothingness compared to the Infinite is the only way to initially understand the Infinite. Thereafter, a methodical approach, starting with acquiring jnana (knowledge and wisdom), will put us on the path of awareness and lead us towards the Infinite. Filling ourselves with jnana to our capacity during this *jivan* (life) should be the goal of every jiva. The adoption of the 10 gunas can accelerate our jnana and take us towards fulfilment. Moksha is when you merge with the Infinite with complete awareness. The different chapters in this book explain this path.

We live in times where time is most precious, and hence, I have kept the book short. And hopefully, you will find the lessons in this book easy to understand and implement in everyday life. Reach out to me if I can help you during this lifetime and for the many lifetimes to come.

Terminology

In the Vedic tradition, God is addressed by many names. He is perceived in many forms. This is done to amplify his infinite traits. In this book, I use terms like the Infinite (*ananta* in Sanskrit) and Universal Intelligence (*sarvajna* in Sanskrit) to emphasize the context. All such terms refer to God.

JNANA

Let There Be Light

The Vedas proclaim that the sound of 'Aum' at the time of creation started the vibration that planted the seed that grew into our universe. In the Old Testament, the Book of Genesis states that at the time of creation, God said, 'Let there be light,' and there was light. Do these two ancient sayings have anything in common? If so, what is the relationship between sound and light? How do these universal happenings affect our everyday life?

The deciphering of these mysterious phenomena could yield clues to existence and the myriad of events that somehow come together to create a path of success.

Bangalore summers in the '50s and '60s were truly wonderful. There were very few artificial lights in those days. Only homes and streets were lit by dim electric bulbs. There was also no pollution to prevent us from sitting outside and staring at the glorious clear blue sky. Thousands of stars twinkled far away, and we were even rewarded with an occasional shooting star. Growing up, my little mind would try to grasp the enormity of the universe and wonder about the One who created all of it. Was it all a mere accidental happening or was it the result of the master plan of a Universal Intelligence? The famous mantra 'Aum Tat Sat' is reality indeed. In this mantra, the wise ones proclaimed 'Oh! That is true.' What is 'That'? It is the creator of the magnificent and unfathomable universe. It is the Infinite, the undefinable source of light that shines through everything. The twinkling stars, as bright as they may be, are so far away that it seems impossible to get rid of the surrounding darkness. The stars are so far away that the very light that I saw on those summer nights had left the stars millions of years ago. How then can this light dispel the darkness around me during my relatively insignificant existence?

Why is darkness so dark anyway? Is it merely the absence of light that is creating the darkness or is it the opposite of light? Why do we fear lurking dangers while in darkness? The answer is that darkness has its own character. It is not merely the absence of light. While light gives us a sense of security, darkness causes insecurity and fear of the unknown. While light can enable us to see the landscape, darkness prevents us from seeing even the immediate surroundings. It is for this reason that we seek light.

While the stars may be too far to give us any significant light, one heavenly body that comes to our rescue is the moon. Moonlight is pleasing, calming and even romantic. However, it is cyclical in nature. What starts off as a mere sliver on the new moon day grows each day till it reaches its full potential on the full moon day. Even though it is only giving us reflected light, it has the ability to to absorb the harshness of the sunlight and share the soothing part of the light with us. One can get sunburnt but not a moon burn. We can stare at the moon directly without any harm to our vision. But it has its flaws on the surface, which are visible even to the naked eye. The moon is closer to the earth and exerts its gravitational pull on our minds.

Then there are the artificial man-made lights, whose glare can hide the stars and render the enchanting moonlight insignificant. These lights, while giving us a false sense of security, make objects appear more exciting than they truly are. Instead of calming the mind, they create stress and induce sleepless nights. They are exhausting and manipulate our senses. They seem to give a false sense of understanding of our surroundings.

There are basically two types of artificial light. The first type of electric light uses a filament. When current passes through it, there is a resistance to the flow of current. This resistance generates heat in the filament, eventually turning the filament red hot or even white hot, thereby emitting light. But in the process of generating this light, it also generates a lot of heat and noise in the surroundings. The second type of artificial light uses an element whose atoms go into an excited state when subjected to a high potential. The life of an excited atom is in nanoseconds. When the excited atom falls back to its normal state, the acquired excess energy is given out in the form of photons, which light up the surroundings.

You may wonder what all of this has to do with success. The answer is: everything. What happens in the macro-universe is reflected in the micro-universe. What happens outside is symbolic of what happens inside you. Careful observation of the outside can help us manage and direct what happens within us.

Light is symbolic of 'jnana'. This Sanskrit word's meaning translates to mean information, knowledge and wisdom, all rolled into one. Even in English, the word used for attaining the state of ultimate knowledge is 'enlightenment'. One of the main Upanishads is called Brihadaranyaka Upanishad. In this work, a famous mantra pleads 'tamaso ma jyotirgamaya', which means 'lead me from darkness to light'. Here, it is not physical light but ultimate wisdom that is being pursued.

Jnana itself comes in three varieties: *yathartha jnana, viparita jnana* and *ajnana*. In a manner of speaking, we can think of the first type as natural light, the second as artificial light and the third as darkness. In Sanskrit, the same word can have different meanings based on the context. In this context, we could think of yathartha jnana as something that is a resource for me to attain success, and viparita jnana as the incorrect or delusional path. In order to attain success, it is imperative that I should be able to differentiate between the three types of jnana and seek only yathartha jnana. The acquired jnana manifests itself in the eventual outcome of life, irrespective of the difficulty or enjoyment along the path. While yathartha jnana leads to upward mobility and bliss, viparita jnana takes us in circles, and ajnana results in downward fall into sorrow and failure.

Every person interested in sadhana, i.e. accomplishment in life, seeks yathartha jnana. I was no exception. But along the way, we get confused and make mistakes. That is not a problem as long as we learn from our mistakes and realign our journey. The bigger question is where does one find this jnana? Of late, we have become enamoured with information, which is so readily available in plenty. We may even confuse this for our own jnana, while surrendering our thoughts and beliefs to those who are providing the information.

So, what is one to do? Where do we search for true knowledge and wisdom that are truly uplifting and resourceful? One approach is to look for those bits of wisdom that have come in the past. Like the stars in the sky, these seemingly eternal bits of wisdom have stood the test of time. There are two problems associated with this process. The first and foremost problem is that of the glare of artificial sources of knowledge, which, like artificial light, can create a lot of noise and unwanted excitement in our lives. The bombardment of data, studies, opinions and other information can overshadow the wisdom of the distant past. One has to learn to completely shut down the consumption of these ever-present bombardments. The second problem is that of understanding. Just as a bright star can appear as a mere twinkling point of light, the amount of knowledge and wisdom that we can glean from these thoughts of the distant past can be limited. This may be due to barriers of language as well as context. This is apparent from the fact that most people who are born and raised in Southeast Asia benefit very little from the Vedas, perhaps the greatest source of all knowledge in the world.

We finally come to that one source that can play a huge role in our journey. That entity is a guru. Unfortunately, this word has often been misused to mean a mystic or a spiritual person who can solve all our problems. Nothing could be farther from the truth. Any person who claims to have all the answers is not being truthful. Just as the moon only reflects the light from the sun, a true guru will only reflect the jnana that can only come from the Infinite, the source of all knowledge and wisdom. This requires that the guru is always exposed to this source. Secondly, just as we do not pay for moonlight, a true guru does not seek to benefit, financially or otherwise, from those who are basking in the calming knowledge and wisdom.

Just as the moon starts as a mere sliver, grows to a full moon and then starts receding, a guru also comes into our lives, grows in stature and fades away. But in the process of doing so, a guru sheds the light of knowledge and wisdom on the landscape of life. This can be enough to find our path and purpose in life to achieve success. However, clouds of doubt and insolence can easily block this great source of knowledge from us.

In my own life, I was truly blessed to come across a true guru. Dr Bannanje Govindacharya, who passed away just a few months ago, neither looked nor behaved like a guru of my imagination. Even though he was one of the greatest scholars of the Vedas in recent times, he was a very humble person. The very first lesson that I learnt from him was that although a seeker of knowledge searches for a guru, it is the guru who identifies the disciple.

It is said that it takes three types of energies to bring success to any endeavour: *ichha shakti*, *jnana shakti* and *kriya shakti*. The first is a firm desire cemented by determination and willpower. We may have that. But only a guru can give us jnana shakti or knowledge. It is not mere words and teachings. Like a funnel, a guru will harness the energy at a higher level and pour it into our intellect. Confusion will be replaced by clarity. Questions will be replaced by answers. Lastly, kriya shakti is the energy that makes everything fall into place. Only God can give us that. It flows in abundance in efforts that are not self-centred but benefits all.

This knowledge and wisdom is the light that the scriptures talk about—the inner light that dismisses any darkness, depression, fear and anxiety from our minds and hearts. I can say that any success I have had is based on the firm foundation of jnana that has been handed down from generation to generation, guru to disciple, from the time of creation, from that seed called 'Aum'.

BHAKTI

We spend so much time and energy in the pursuit of pleasure and happiness. When we are not satisfied with one thing, we chase another. Our minds get immersed in the thought of possessing an object, an idea or a person. These thoughts can direct our speech and action. It can become an obsession. That is not passion.

The problem with going after sensory pleasures is that it is fleeting. And it always comes at a price.

More often than not, the price we pay is too high for the need it may satisfy. Moreover, the craving still remains. It is a never-ending process of going after something, and unless done as a part of a bigger goal, it will always fall short of our expectations.

This inability of sensory pleasures to satisfy a craving can only lead to negative feelings. To start with, the craving can cloud our judgement, and we may end up doing things that we regret later. We may also get angry when we are denied what we want. The absence of an object or a person can cause depression. None of these negative feelings can lead us on the path to success.

Then, there is the pursuit of happiness. Even though it may not be as fleeting as sensory pleasures, it cannot give us permanent escape from the daily sufferings of drudgery. It can indeed elevate us to a higher plane but will also let us down after a while. While no serious negative outcomes may arise, it may not be a permanent solution to our lack of success in reaching a desired goal.

What we actually aspire for, whether we are aware of it or not, is bliss. This is the elevated state that comes only from resourceful knowledge and wisdom.

It is an inner awareness that is not affected by external happenings. It is a state in which we are immersed in the consciousness of the Universal Intelligence. The focus on the Infinite alone leads to reverential passion and passionate reverence. It is the purest form of love, with no expectations. No worldly difficulty can cause internal suffering. The pursuit of this pure passion is what is called 'bhakti' in Sanskrit.

Age and Passion

For most of us, it is difficult to acquire jnana and develop bhakti at a young age. During teen years, most people expect perfection from an imperfect world. This disparity between expectation and reality induces rebellion. The rebellious mind leads to reckless speech and action.

To overcome these harmful outcomes, two constraints can come to the rescue. The first one is what we call *sanskar* in Sanskrit. This word is often translated as tradition, but it is more than tradition. It is not only what flows in our blood due to genetic influence but also the baggage we bring into each life from our previous lives. Baggage need not always be negative. We may also be born with jnana and bhakti, which serve as the starting point. So, we need not get frustrated with limited accomplishment in any life, as the outcome is the integration of our actions in many lives.

The second constraint comes from society itself. If we are surrounded by activities that are conducive to acquiring real knowledge, the chances of us being naturally drawn towards it are higher. So, the leaders in society may be those who have administrative and leadership skills. But these leaders should be guided by the wise, whose sole agenda is the preservation and dissemination of yathartha jnana.

Distractions

It is only natural that we encounter distractions along the path. Our senses and mind are constantly scanning our surroundings. It is a tool for survival. We should be able to sense danger and predators in our surroundings.

However, we need not get distracted and drift away from the path to our destination. There is a wonderful story in the Puranas about a young man called Ajamila. He belonged to a religious family that practised strict rules of behaviour. One day, he went to the forest to gather flowers for his daily worship. While wandering in the forest, he came across a very beautiful woman of questionable character. He got so enamoured by her looks that he forgot about his family back home and spent many decades with this woman, totally engrossed in sensory pleasures. In old age, while on his deathbed, he called for his son, who was named after God. Hearing this, the angels of God came and rescued him from his predicament. After this, Ajamila realized his mistakes, returned to a spiritual path and finally attained the state of ultimate fulfilment—salvation.

There are several lessons to be learnt from this story. The young Ajamila had sanskar. But it was one of religious restriction rather than spiritual passion. So, he was easily distracted by worldly pleasures. But he also had inner knowledge, which saved him in the end. While we may not be subjected to such extreme situations, we are distracted by smaller attractions. The only thing that can bring us back on track is our inner love, reverence and passion for the Eternal Truth. This Eternal Truth is what is collectively called the Vedas, which contain knowledge of both the creator and his creation.

The Journey

Normally, every journey has a beginning and an end. There is a starting point and a destination. We are accustomed to taking breaks in a long journey. But our focus is always on the destination and remaining distance. It is only natural that we try to apply the same rules to our lives. We think of birth as the starting point and death as the end point. In between, we set goals and try to reach them. Seldom do we wonder what our final destination is. We become obsessed with the intermediate goals and become passionate about reaching these goals. If we do not succeed in reaching them, we get angry and frustrated. If we manage to reach them, after the initial excitement, we become dissatisfied with them and start searching for new goals. And this becomes a pattern. In the last stages of our lives, we remain internally dissatisfied while externally boasting about our accomplishments.

So, what is the real journey? What intermediate

goals do I set for myself? When will I ever reach my true destination? To answer these questions, one has to realize that the only goal that can be truly satisfying is when the journey itself is the destination. Once we are on this eternal journey, we have reached our destination and we will be satisfied. But if we ever stop thinking that we have reached the destination, we are no longer at the destination. Such a journey would be possible only when we embark on reaching the Infinite.

So, every goal becomes a mere break in the eternal journey. No matter what I do, the focus is on the Infinite and not the short-term goal. Life itself becomes a small part of this journey. If I do not reach a short-term goal, it is perhaps due to the fact that it is not on the real path. Obsessions or negative emotions, such as frustration, disappointment and depression, do not make way for passionate reverence or true bhakti.

My Journey

If I had known all this when I was a teenager or even in my 20s, my journey might not have been any different. But it would have definitely been less stressful and more blissful. As I look back, I wonder why failure in reaching a certain goal did not really cause me any anguish. I just kept going, and here I am today, in a sweet spot. Perhaps, at a subconscious level, I knew some things that I was not even aware of on the surface.

I don't recall anyone asking me what I wanted to be when I grew up. It never occurred to me to ask the question myself. It was a carefree existence. My first passion was the NCC in high school. I joined the naval wing of the NCC. The white uniform was fascinating.

I spent the next six years with a passionate zeal for joining the Indian Navy. My uniform was always the whitest and best-starched. My shoes were always the shiniest. I could rattle off the names of all the different types of ships and what they did. I could tie all the rope knots. I was the best cadet. But it all seemed a waste when I failed the medical exam to become a naval pilot. But that training was not really wasted. I learnt discipline. I learnt leadership qualities. I learnt to interact with people from places and background far different than mine.

I tasted the sweet expanse of the sea. I learnt to imagine what was beyond the horizon and travel towards it, imbued with the spirit of exploration. These qualities have helped in all stages of my life.

I had to start all over again. In my early 20s, when I landed in New York with $8 and a dream, I had no idea about all the struggles that awaited me. While my former classmates were in graduate studies, I was taking courses to get an associate degree in engineering technology. While they spent their evenings in advanced studies, I was sweeping floors and emptying trash cans.

But I was trained to be passionate. My floors were always the cleanest when I was a janitor. My trash cans always had fresh liners. I took pride in what I was doing. I was a janitor for almost two years. I was not ashamed of what I was doing. I enjoyed everything I ate because it was the result of hard work. I learnt to respect those who work hard but are seldom noticed. A few years ago, I came out of my office at the university to go home in the evening. A janitor was mopping the floor. He stopped and said, 'It is OK, sir. You can go.' I smiled and said, 'No, I will wait till it is dry.' I knew what it feels like when someone walks on a wet floor that you have just mopped. A lesson you cannot learn unless you mop floors for a living.

Many years went by. Many goals achieved and many hurdles crossed. In my professional career, I went on to work as a technician for several years, which allowed me to get an engineering degree, with no support from anyone. I got a master's degree as well. I worked as an engineer for a few years. I went back to the university to get a PhD. For more than three decades, I worked as a professor. The US government and industry gave me millions of dollars to do research in engineering. I educated thousands of students.

Not only my professional life but my family also grew. My spiritual life reached levels that I was not even aware of. It is a journey. And there is no end to it because it is all a path towards the Infinite. In Sankrit, the word *gati* describes both the destination and the journey. And a reverential passion towards both the path and the destination is a necessary requirement. And that comes only from true knowledge and wisdom.

VAIRAGYA

It is indeed a wonder that most of us love to be attached to many objects, people and ideas, and yet aspire to be free to live as we wish. Every attachment seems wonderful when we are unattached, while freedom seems wonderful when we are attached. The eternal question is: how to enjoy the pleasures of attachment and yet experience the bliss of freedom?

From the time we are born, we seek attachment to our mothers for sheer survival. We seek this attachment intuitively and unknowingly for both sustenance and protection. Then comes our attachment to our fathers and other members of our family. These bonds can become very strong and cause tremendous grief when eventually broken, as all bonds are.

As we get older and the hormones kick in, we cannot wait to form relationships with others. When new families are created and children are born, they can become the centre of our universe. As they grow into adulthood, we also move towards old age. In the process, we would have spent an enormous amount of time, energy and resources in maintaining and sustaining these bonds.

Then, there are friends. The very definition of a friend seems to change over time. As children, anyone who is willing to play with us is a friend. In youth, anyone who will give us company in our adventures is a friend. In adulthood, anyone who comes to our rescue in times of need is a friend. The common theme is: it based on self-centred expectation. As our needs change, so does our selection of friends. We detach ourselves from friendships as easily as we get attached to them.

Ideas and Intellect

As if our attachments to people are not enough, we get attached to ideas of right and wrong as well. These ideas can be due to our own nature or superimposed by others. Either way, once percolated through our minds, the ideas get cemented in the intellect, making it very difficult to shake off.

The attachment to ideas can sometimes be extreme. People can even go as far as to harm others to prove that their ideas are right. In reality, it proves nothing. It is only a disturbing and dangerous trend when our attachment to an idea, belief or a concept is so strong that it can harm others who may not have similar ideas.

Detachment

Two people who like each other might hold hands while strolling. But it would be foolish for the same people to glue their hands together. When glued hands have to be unglued out of necessity, the skin is going to tear, resulting in a wound and an eventual scar.

To strongly attach myself to any person, object or an idea, mentally or emotionally, would be equally foolish. I should know the end result will be hurt and pain. This does not preclude from being in close contact and enjoying the company of the desired object. But the separation can be easy and harmless.

This type of detached attachment is highly advocated in Vedic philosophy and is called 'vairagya'. Just as a swan can easily swim in water and not get wet and drown because of its smooth feathers and an oily secretion from its glands that forms a layer, a wise person wears detachment as a layer protecting him from excessive attachment. The only path that can help us master this state of vairagya is one of jnana and bhakti for something bigger and grander than everything around us.

The Elephant and the Crocodile

There is a beautiful story in the Srimad Bhagavata Purana, written by Veda Vyasa more than five thousand years ago. On the surface, the story appears pointless. But on closer examination, we find a fabulous lesson for all mankind. It teaches us the outcome of a life dedicated to mere enjoyment, and the path that will lead to liberation from the clutches of a purely materialistic pursuit.

The story goes like this. Once upon a time, there lived an elephant called Gajendra. The very name Gajendra means the 'king among elephants'. This elephant had a loving family and was enjoying a pleasant, carefree life. One day, Gajendra set out to have a little fun. His companion female elephant and the kid elephants all followed the leader.

The herd was wandering around the palace of Devendra, the lord of all divine entities who control our five sensory organs and five action-oriented senses. Gajendra noticed a charming lake with exquisite lotus flowers on the surface. He decided to enjoy the water and stepped into the lake. The other elephants followed Gajendra into the water. They started playing and throwing water on each other with their trunks.

But there was danger lurking beneath the surface. Unknown to the elephants, there was a crocodile in the depths of the lake. While the elephants were enjoying themselves, the crocodile quietly came and caught Gajendra's leg. Gajendra, arrogant about his size and strength, was not overly bothered by the crocodile. He tried to shake it off. But to his surprise, the crocodile was strong and would not let go of his leg. Gajendra tried with all his might, but to no avail. Then he started loudly trumpeting in pain. Seeing this, all the other elephants rushed to his rescue. But even this did not help. Unable to help in any way, all the other elephants walked away.

The lonely Gajendra was getting desperate. He could not think of any escape. He noticed a lotus flower in the lake. He plucked it with his trunk, looked above and held the flower up as an offering to God. Then he started praying with utmost passion. Upon hearing the sincere prayers of Gajendra, Lord Vishnu came down to rescue him. Using his chakra, he struck the crocodile and killed it. Out of the body of the crocodile, a Gandharva (musicians of God; in this case, belonging to Devendra's kingdom) emerged. He narrated how he had been cursed to live in the body of a crocodile. He thanked Lord Vishnu for his deliverance from the lowly life and disappeared.

Even Gajendra was rewarded for his jnana and bhakti with ultimate fulfilment—eternal salvation.

The Lesson

At the outset, this story might sound pointless since tuskers are solitary creatures who seldom wander in herds. Moreover, an elephant plucking a flower, offering it to God and chanting prayers seems a fantasy. If that is all we get from the story, we are truly missing the critical lesson.

The elephant is merely symbolic. It is actually a story about us. The very word *gaja* for elephant in Sanskrit can be split into two parts: *ga* and *ja*. Sanskrit is an etymological language, and every consonant has a root meaning. Several root meanings can exist for the same consonant, and we have to pick the correct meaning based on the context. In the present context, 'ga' could mean 'to go' and 'ja' could mean 'to be born'. So, gaja is someone whose karma or actions only lead to rebirth. That is a reference to humans, who perform karma that only leads to rebirth. And the whole story is about how to escape this eternal cycle.

On a different note, just like a big elephant sauntering about, we, too, go through life as if it is never-ending. We are also overly impressed with our own strength and ability to ward off debilitating dangers lurking unseen. We get attached to our families and tend to spend all our time and energy in the enjoyment of their company. Even though it is natural for us to be close to our family members, it would be unwise to think that they can always get us out of difficult situations.

The lake with the lotus flowers represents the world of sensory enjoyment for us. While it is not wrong to enjoy the material comforts that we are blessed with, it would be foolish to be unaware of the dangers that are present in such indulgences. The real danger is in our getting attached to sensory enjoyment and mistaking recreation for a need. Once we get caught in the clutches of this obsession, not even our family or well-wishers can save us.

Once caught in the grip of the crocodile, Gajendra was no longer enjoying the company of his family. The enchanting surroundings also did not seem to make a difference. Similarly, undue attachments only lead to pain and suffering.

Desperation sets in. The lotus represents the universe in Vedic symbolism. In our own little universe, there are many things within our reach. Many of these objects are beautiful, soft and fragrant, just like the lotus flower. All we can do is to offer all our karma to God.

In the story, Vishnu appears mounted on his *vahana* Garuda and destroys the crocodile with his chakra. There is symbolism embedded here as well. Garuda represents Vedic knowledge, and the chakra represents dharma or righteous living. So, when we go through life with detached attachment to our surroundings and look at everything as an offering, Vedic wisdom will come to our rescue. All pain and suffering will be destroyed by dharma.

Vairagya and I

I have had my share of temptations. At times, I have succumbed to them. In such cases, the end result has always been pain and suffering. But many of these were short-lived and inconsequential. As silly and strange as it may sound, one thing that I have struggled with all my life has been attachment to good food. As much as I try to not pay attention, even the sight and smell of tasty food is tempting. And decades of indulgence has resulted in health issues.

I am sure that we all have our weaknesses. After all, we are human. Unlike animals, who indulge in sensory pleasures for a purpose in a limited manner, human indulgence is mainly for the sake of pleasure and has no boundaries. About 20 years ago, I decided to follow the religious practice of complete fasting on the eleventh day of each half-cycle of the lunar month. Initially, it was not only difficult mentally but also physically. But once I got into the habit, I found it exhilarating. It was almost as if I was freed from the clutches of food. I still enjoy good food, but I am no longer a slave to it.

That is not the only attachment I had to shake off. But with each object and incident, I learnt that it is possible to experience the positive side of anything and it is not necessary to attach myself to a specific outcome. Most attachments are mental, and the mind is a creature of habit. I have personally found that all attachments are detachable when we focus on the Infinite and align all pleasures as offerings to Him.

PRAGNYA

The Sanskrit word 'pragnya' could be crudely translated as 'the ability to know ahead of an event'. The ability of some people to properly evaluate the present and accurately predict an outcome in the future is not easy or common. Yet, many successful people seem to have an uncanny ability to do just that. This allows them to plan for the future and proactively deal with unfavourable outcomes. That, obviously, will allow them to minimize the harm from unfavourable events and outcomes. In chapter 2 of the Bhagavad Gita, Arjuna asks the same question to Shri Krishna. He asks how one gets a stable pragnya and what the characteristics of a person with steady pragnya are. Shri Krishna replies that the one who is not unduly occupied with sensory pleasures will have a steady pragnya. Further, he says that such a person will possess awareness of the self. And the awareness has to extend to our surroundings as well.

Awareness

There are three states of existence. We can be awake, asleep or in a dream state. When we are awake, all our sensory organs collect information, and the mind processes it in real time. When the mind has any question, it consults the intellect before inferring anything. In the sleep state, the mind disconnects from active processing of incoming data from the sensory organs but can still be interrupted by any unusual or dangerous happenings in our surroundings. In the dream state, even though the real sensory inputs are not fed to the mind, our memory feeds data to the mind, sometimes in a disconnected fashion. The mind reacts to this data as if it is coming from the senses.

It would seem logical, under these normal circumstances, that we would be aware of our surroundings and happenings. Yet, we find that we do not remember witnessing something that would have happened right in front of our eyes. This is because we are not attentive enough to keep our minds focused on the senses. We get bored and let the mind wander in memory land, focusing on people, objects or ideas that we are attached to. We start to daydream. This lack of awareness in the physical world can cause great harm in our perception of events and people.

A person aiming to succeed in reaching a goal should not only know how to get there, be passionate about the goal and be detached from the outcome of karma while performing it, but he should also be constantly aware of the present and not daydream about the future.

Saakshi

We often hear of a sixth sense or intuition. What exactly is it and can it be trusted? To understand this 'sixth sense', we need to understand the normal process. The perception of our surroundings and the happenings are processed by the mind. The *manas* (mind) looks to the *buddhi* (intellect) for resolution of any confusion in the processed data. The rules used by the intellect are derived from prior experiences. It is difficult to process a brand new experience without prior knowledge.

To overcome this difficulty, we are all blessed with this sixth sense or *saakshi* that keeps a check on the buddhi and prevents it from arriving at the wrong conclusion. The problem is that the intellect resists the input from saakshi, since it may not agree with its own conclusions. Generally, females are supposed to have higher intuition, and males are blessed with higher intellect. In the Vedic tradition, a balance between the intellect and intuition is highly recommended. This is symbolically represented in the Ardhanarishvara form of Shiva. Since Shiva has control over the mind, he is depicted as half-male and half-female in this form.

The Chakra

According to Patanjali's *Yoga Shastra*, there are several energy centres in the human body that can perform amazing functions when activated. One of these energy centres is located at the level of the brain. It emanates energy from the middle of the forehead, i.e. the 'third eye' chakra. It is also capable of receiving energy in the form of guidance from the divine forces in the universe.

So, what does this so-called third eye see? If it is capable of receiving guidance, then who is constantly watching us to offer guidance? And how can we trust this unknown and unseen source?

To understand the concept of this chakra, we should first realize that nobody is stalking our thoughts and activities. However, the universe is a repository of collective knowledge and wisdom. It is stored in *akasha* or the space, which is filled with energy. Even though it is not simple or easy to extract the needed wisdom, just the very act of keeping the third eye open is important. As with any type of extraordinary accomplishment, the path to success is slow but rewarding.

Height and Sight

It is obvious that a tall person can see a little farther than a shorter person. This is true both physically and metaphorically. But when we want to see farther than what we are naturally endowed with, we don't try to become taller. On the contrary, we know that we have to stand at a height. The climb can be stressful and tiring. The height may be dizzying and scary, but there is no alternative to elevation to see the whole landscape.

It is not mere knowledge or even wisdom that can elevate us to greater heights. But deep meditation or *tapas*, can lift us to great heights. From this vantage point, we can clearly see the landscape of our lives, both in terms of time and space. The ability to envision all events in our lives, in the context of our past and future, can suddenly provide clarity. Our lives become simpler, meaningful and more blissful.

Who Am I?

That, as they say, is the million-dollar question.
Even though one could take this question to a very
deep and spiritual level, we will keep our discussion
to a somewhat simple and earthly level. Our own
perception of who we are as human beings keeps
changing. We keep looking in the mirror of society
to figure out who we are and what we look like.
Therein lies the problem. As times change and
our surroundings alter, we are told different things
about ourselves. We start believing it. And then,
a new set of people come and tell us that we are
something else. We gloat at times, and get depressed
at other times. All because others are defining who
we are.

More often than not, what we hear from others
is expressed in the form of a compliment or a
slur. That actually does not change who we are,
but it can definitely change who we think we are.
Only a malleable mind can be shaped by someone
else. An honest contemplation of our strengths and
weaknesses can give us a much clearer image of our
true character.

Judging Others

Unfortunately, our awareness of people and their agenda is often limited to what we hear and see. A good-looking stranger is more likely to elicit a smile than someone who is not quite that physically attractive. Furthermore, when others tell us something, we often take it at face value. When someone does something, we think as to why we would do the same thing if we were to do it. We attach our motivation to someone else's action, without having a clue about the motivation of others. We make judgements. We get close to some people and stay far away from some others, all based on our judgements. And sometimes, to our dismay, we find out later that our initial opinions and judgements were not correct.

This is where our saakshi or the sixth sense can come into play. In most cases, we are more likely to consult other people than trust our own intuition. Development of a healthy intuition takes effort. Like anything else, we have to allow intuition the space to grow. It has to be nurtured and protected. It has to be trusted and respected. When developed properly, it can actually help us see through the smokescreen.

What Did I Do?

We seldom wonder about our roles in what we think, say or do. If it is something creditworthy, we are quick to claim credit. If it is something not desirable, we are equally quick to shift the blame and lament about our lack of control over the situation. But we cannot have it both ways. Which is it? Were we the 'doers' and deserve credit or was it beyond our control and we do not deserve discredit? The answers to these questions are clearly there in Vedic tradition. But to understand the answers and use them for the benefit of both ourselves and those around us, we need both knowledge and faith.

In Vedic tradition, we have the responsibility for the intent. Our teachers get the credit for teaching us how to do things. But the most important part is the enabling energy that is given to us (or denied) based on our nature and karma. There is an entire hierarchy of divine entities who control the functioning of every part of our body and mind.

By having the right intent and seeking the blessings of the correct *devata* or divine being, we can end up with the ability to do things that are beyond the normal. This is not mythology but verifiable knowledge.

My Experience

Many of my experiences in this domain seem unreal. But they were real. I distinctly remember a few incidents from my childhood. When I was hardly five years old, my parents would discuss some issue in my presence, thinking that I would not understand, since it was only for 'grown-ups'. But I would clearly see through the situation and know the actual facts. But I did not know how to express myself. Neither did I have the courage to do so. But in retrospect, I was almost always right.

Much later, when I was an adult, I could very easily make out when people were saying one thing while thinking something else. I would almost get tempted to ask why someone was lying. But since I could never explain how I knew the truth, I always had to keep it to myself.

Even in certain situations that were dangerous, I have asked for help from above. Almost always, the situation would change. At first, I would think that it was mere coincidence. Over time, I have realized that nothing is random. Luck has no meaning. The closest word for it in Sanskrit is *adrishta*, which literally means 'something that cannot be seen'. It is the unseen hand that can guide us and protect us, only if we have faith in it.

MEDHA SHAKTI

Every action has a reaction. Even when our reaction to an external event is not physical or verbal, it will at least be mental. Our observation is based on perception. What we perceive, in terms of the five senses of perception, is retained in the memory of our brain while it is being processed. The mind comes up with a holistic image of an event. Whether we react to this or not depends on its relevance to us, as dictated by the intellect.

This process is not too far from the way a

computer processes data. Inputs from one or more sources are stored in a cache memory while it is being processed by the Common Procurement Vocabulary (CPV). Whether results are merely displayed or stored permanently in the hard drive depends on the algorithm and, of course, the human input.

According to Vedic philosophy, human beings have the equivalent of the hard drive as well. In Sanskrit, it is called *chitta* (the memory shell surrounding the jiva). It is this chitta that informs our *chetana* or consciousness. The important question is: what exactly gets stored and what does it take to recall the stored knowledge?

Unlike a computer's hard drive, the chitta is a memory shell that is almost permanently attached to the jiva or the soul. This enables the jiva to traverse through multiple lives and integrate the knowledge and wisdom acquired through all experiences in all our lives.

If the brain starts to lose its memory strength, we may become forgetful. But if we lose the connection to the chitta, we cannot recall past experiences. It should not come as a surprise then that the most recent experiences are at the top, which we can recall with relative ease. As time passes, our experiences get buried deeper in memory. However, all experiences are connected to other similar experiences, and these connections can jog our past while we observe the present.

Our ability to see the connections and recall the relevant past is called 'medha shakti' in Sanskrit. This is an extremely important trait in a person. It enables us to make good decisions in the present, based on our knowledge of the past. The greater the medha shakti, the deeper we can dig into the past and the faster we can recall.

Observation

We often see but do not observe. We hear but do not listen. We touch but do not feel. The reason for this is our disconnecting the mind from the inputs received from our sensory organs. We are not interested in the happenings around us. The mind will be engaged in something from the past or daydreaming about the future.

We get disinterested because we feel that the

happenings do not concern our well-being. We react only when we feel that something might affect us. This is not a wise approach. We can never actually know how something can affect us in the future. But there is something even more important. We can learn a lot from the experiences of others.

Even though we may not fully relate to the experiences of others, we can certainly learn something from what others are going through. This can help us deal with similar situations in the future.

Conclusions

Every time we hear something or see something, we draw a conclusion. This conclusion may be reached after careful thought or be reactive in nature. Either way, the conclusions are only as good as the basis on which the conclusions are drawn. And as all other aspects of karma, this, too, depends on the knowledge and wisdom that one has accumulated over many a lifetimes. Based on the outcomes, we might have drawn different conclusions about similar situations. But if we are unable to make proper connections between differing conclusions, the experiences of the past cannot help us in dealing with the present.

Advantages

A person who is blessed with good medha shakti is called a *medhavi*. Such a person can be identified as having many of the leadership qualities that most people can only aspire to.

Perhaps the most enviable trait is the ability to view everything from a multidimensional viewpoint. Every situation in life is complex. Multiple facets define such situations. Yet, we mostly view it from a singular perspective. An individual with medha shakti can view the situation from many angles simultaneously. Obviously, this gives the person a much better understanding of the situation and its possible outcomes.

The second visible trait is above-normal intelligence. In general, we can define intelligence as the ability to come up with the correct answer to a given problem. With greater intelligence, one can come up with the correct solution in a shorter amount of time. If we can recall a past experience with similar context, it takes us a shorter amount of time to arrive at the correct answer.

Impromptu speech is a wonderful ability to have. A medhavi can speak effectively on a wide range of topics, with no preparation. Such a person does not search for ideas or words. There are no breaks and awkward silences in his speech. There is a forceful energy behind his words and gestures. This ability comes from the power to recall stored data in real time.

Fear comes from unknown outcomes in the future. The ability to predict outcomes allows us to plan for all possible outcomes, even if some of the outcomes are unwanted or undesirable. The knowledge of possible outcomes allows a medhavi to take risks without fear.

There is an interesting concept called *dharana* in Sanskrit. This is the process of intense concentration of the mind on something, where we can actually become the object temporarily. This would allow us to read others' mind and actually feel what they are feeling. This not only gives a medhavi the power of empathy but also the strength to understand others, even if they do not share their inner thoughts.

Improving Medha Shakti

Even though it is not possible to develop medha shakti in a short amount of time, it is essential to be aware of it. Furthermore, we can make a sincere attempt to improve certain aspects of it.

The first step is to observe happenings in our surroundings. Most important things are present in subtleties. So, paying close attention is the key to catching these subtle facets of any situation. But we usually observe only the gross happenings. So, fine-tuning our senses and mind is the first step.

Secondly, we need to view happenings from multiple viewpoints. This is easier said than done. We need to learn the psychology of others involved in any situation. We need to make an attempt to understand the context and background of other people. Gradually, we will learn to see their viewpoints as well. This will not only help us in obtaining a holistic view of the situation but also build empathy for other valid viewpoints.

Third, effort has to be made to improve focus and concentration. Concentrating on a focal point is like a drill that can go deep. We need the depth of understanding, not mere perception. In this regard, meditation on a regular basis helps us in improving our concentration.

Fourth, our intellect needs to be very sharp. It is intellect that helps the mind in drawing conclusions. But the intellect needs a set of rules to go by. Instead of relying on what others tell us, we can rely on our own past experiences to guide the intellect. Initially, we can just rely on our experiences in the present life. As we go farther back, gradually our intellect learns to go deeper and discover a treasure trove of experiences from even before we were born.

Lastly, we can practise impromptu speeches on a given topic. This can start as simple attempts, talking for a few minutes on general topics. As we gradually progress, both in duration and complexity, we suddenly find that we know many things that we were not even aware of.

In conclusion, it is true that having medha

shakti is indeed a blessing. But it is important to understand what it is and make a sincere attempt to improve the foundational traits that can lead to the development and improvement of this very valuable trait.

DHRITI

All the concepts explained in this chapter are components of a root trait called 'dhriti' in Sanskrit. This trait is best explained by looking at a story from the great epic Srimad Bhagavata Purana. The story is about a five-year-old boy named Dhruva and his spiritual journey.

According to the story, there once lived a king called Uttanapada. He had two wives named Suneeti and Suruchi. Suneeti had a five-year-old son named Dhruva, and Suruchi had a little son named Uttama. Between the two wives, Uttanapada favoured his younger wife, Suruchi.

One day, the king was spending time with Suruchi and Uttama, when Dhruva happened to pass by and saw Uttama sitting on the king's lap. Dhruva asked the king if he, too, could sit on the king's lap. At this, Suruchi got upset and asked Dhruva to go away. She further said that Dhruva should ask God if he could be born as Suruchi's son so that he is able to sit on the king's lap. Suneeti consoled her son but was unable to find a solution.

Dhruva then set out to find God and ask him the question. He went into a forest and performed severe penance. He was guided by the celestial poet-saint Narada. Pleased with Dhruva's austere penance for six months, Vishnu appeared in front of Dhruva, blessed him and granted him all his wishes.

The reason Dhruva succeeds in the end is his confidence in divine fairness. To accomplish his goal, he was ready to make sacrifices, go through difficulties and not give up on his goal. His single-minded focus, determination and fortitude all exemplify the trait of dhriti.

All the names used in the story have meanings that tell their own story. Uttanapada means 'elevated feet'. Not to be taken literally, it refers to a person who is actually spiritually elevated. Suneeti means 'good character' and Suruchi means 'good taste'. So, even the spiritually transcended Uttanapada is attracted to the beauty of Suruchi, as compared to the good character of Suneeti. Uttama means 'superior', while Dhruva means 'permanence'. So, while status can give temporary elevation, the permanence of fortitude will always lead to success. All the traits that we discuss in this chapter, starting from correct knowledge, will bring us the permanence of confidence, patience and fortitude.

Confidence

The path to success is indeed a long and arduous one. We can obtain something temporary, relatively easily. However, accomplishing permanent success in all aspects of life is much more difficult. One can easily lose confidence in a just and equitable universe, when faced with difficulty. But confidence, both within and without, is an essential trait in a person seeking success.

The starting point is the knowledge that leads us to define our goal and come up with a plan of action. But in the process, we can start obsessing about the goal and ignore the path. This lack of focus can blind us from the many pitfalls that are present in any path. And every time we fall, our confidence starts fading.

Self-confidence is a virtue that is often touted as the main source of confidence. However, we should have realistic faith in our abilities. We should also be aware of our weaknesses and come up with a course of action for overcoming our shortfalls. But even under the best of circumstances, if we fail at something in spite of a confident effort, we have the tendency to blame 'luck'. But luck implies randomness, implying little or no connection between effort and outcome.

Then, we place our confidence in the goodness of others. Again, we find that many people are self-centred. They barely care about fairness, unless it suits their convenience. Experiences like these can lead to cynicism. This could even prevent us from putting in the required efforts in reaching our goals.

So, what should we have confidence in? Is there anything that is capable of ensuring fairness in this world? The answer is: the theory of karma. The Vedic thought accepts the presence of an all-knowing Universal Intelligence. This all-powerful and all-pervasive entity keeps track of every single thought, speech and action of every individual. This can appear mind-boggling to us. But it is the very foundation on which the entire Vedic thought is built. We may have to be patient to see the connections between efforts and outcomes. But by developing a strong sense of confidence in the presence of the eternal memory of the Universal Intelligence, we can attain the needed confidence to put in our best efforts, without obsessing about the outcome.

Patience

We are always in a hurry for things to happen, especially those things that we work for. But events have different outcomes at different times, based on the context. So, learning to wait for results to appear at the right time is a strength. This would result from our faith in that everything in the universe is directed by a master plan that we may be incapable of comprehending.

Even though we may understand this concept, the implementation is not easy. When we do not see the desired outcome, we start getting afraid that the outcome may be a failure. The solution to this problem is to focus on the task rather than the outcome. This has been beautifully taught by Shri Krishna in verse 47 of chapter 2 of the Bhagavad Gita.

This verse has been usually translated as 'you have right to perform karma, but not to its fruits.' This might bring up the question: why should I do anything if I don't have the right to the fruits of my labour? That is indeed a valid question. The verse is slightly misunderstood. Once a karma is performed, its results are guaranteed, whether one has a right to it or not. The correct interpretation can be 'you have the right to perform karma, but not to question the timing of the outcome.'

The same verse also warns us against inaction.

We should learn to wait for the fruits of our labour. But we should not wait for the outcome before taking the next step. When climbing a mountain, we should not stop after each step and look towards the peak to see if we have reached it. The focus should be just on the next step. We will know when we have reached the peak.

I have had many personal experiences that have tested my patience. Perhaps the best example is my engineering education. I was 22 years old when I started my engineering education, much later than my peers. By patiently going for one degree after another, I ended up getting my PhD in engineering. But getting my degrees later than normal did not hamper my success. On the contrary, being more mature than my peers by the time I stared pursuing engineering, I actually did better than them.

Fortitude

The hard path to success is often dotted with adversity. It is often essential, as the common saying goes, to 'hang in there'. What is the worst thing that can happen? We may fail at reaching our goal. But we really do not know what is ahead. By giving up prematurely, we are only ensuring failure.

One specific incident from my student days stands out in my memory. When I was an undergraduate student at the University of Tennessee, I always used to envy many of my peers. They were a few years younger. Their tuition, dormitory and food expenses were all taken care of, usually by their parents. All they had to do was study. But I had to work three or four part-time jobs on campus to support myself. I tried to look for technician jobs that paid a little more than other jobs. Even though some juggling was involved, I usually came up with enough money every semester to pay my tuition and maintain some semblance of living, even if it was at a mere poverty level.

So, things were going well until disaster struck in the second semester of my junior year. Suddenly, I lost two of my part-time jobs. Usually, this would not rattle me. I would find something else within a week or two. But to my dismay, weeks went by and I could not find anything. My biggest worry was not living expenses. My roommate, may God bless him, told me that he would manage the rent by himself for a month or two. My big worry was the tuition fees for the following semester.

True to my fears, the next semester arrived, and I had no money to pay the fees. I went to the registrar and poured out my sob story. He was sympathetic but could only give me a two-week extension. So, I went to the director of international student affairs. He, too, was sympathetic but could not find a solution. By all accounts, I should have panicked.

But I kept studying and continued looking for jobs. I had confidence that something would happen. I felt that hard work, sincerity and faith would prevail. After a few days, I got a message that the same director wanted to meet me. I went to see him and was met with a huge smile. He gave me a cheque that covered two semesters' tuition. I was dumbfounded. When I recovered, I asked him where it had come from. He told me that an alumnus of the university had come forward to help me. He wanted to do it anonymously. Even to this day, I do not know who my benefactor was. I made a promise to my benefactor in a letter that I would succeed in life and help deserving students. Fortunately, I have been able to keep my promise. Such experiences not only increase our self-confidence but also our faith in the fairness of the universe.

STITHI

There are over a billion people who identify as Hindu. Very few of them, if any, have chosen Hinduism as a way of life after careful study. They were just born into a 'Hindu' family and grew up to be a Hindu adult. Some of these people blindly follow some rituals, chanting things in an unknown language. At some point, they give up on these as well. Some stick to it, mainly because they want to stick to something. They want to have faith in a higher power. Even though there are always exceptions, most Hindus receive no formal education about their faith at home, school or the temple. Oddly enough, the word 'Hindu' does not even show up in any of the Hindu scriptures. Not in the Vedas. Not in the Puranas. Not even in the Mahabharata or the Ramayana. It was a word coined by alien cultures to fit a glorious and sophisticated way of life into narrowly defined dogma and religion. How can this lead to strong convictions and strength in our values and beliefs, which is our 'stithi'?

Yet, in any Vedic observance, spirituality plays a very important role. This could be a wedding, moving into a newly built home and any personal or social event. On such occasions, the priest performing the puja asks the people offering the puja to do a *sankalpa* (statement of intent or vow stating the purpose of puja being performed). Unfortunately, in many instances, people repeat what the priest says in Sanskrit, without truly understanding what is being said.

Almost always, the stated outcomes of any activity are four-fold: dharma, *artha*, *kama* and moksha, loosely translated as 'righteousness', 'resources', 'desires' and 'eternal fulfilment', respectively. The big question here is whether these outcomes desired are truly heartfelt and stem from strong belief. If that were the case, it would be fairly obvious in our thoughts, actions and speech.

We need to seriously ponder over whether these are strongly held beliefs that we are willing to abide by. In Vedic culture, these beliefs were the very foundations on which society was built. They have served us well, both at societal and individual levels, through good times and difficult times. It has been the resting place for our karma for thousands of years.

Our Tune

We do not know the actual origin of classical music in Vedic culture. But it has certainly been around for thousands of years. Krishna plays the flute, Saraswati plays the veena and Shiva, the damaru. One entire section of the Vedas is set to music— Sama Veda.

Music is an interplay of seven primary notes abbreviated as Sa, Re, Ga, Ma, Pa, Da and Ni. The ascending and descending order of the notes, and the transition between notes define the raga. The raga is more than the tune. It has the power to invoke different emotions in a listener. But as a skilled musician weaves a web of magic with notes, it always comes back to one note—the *sthayi*.

In life, too, it is essential to have a resting place where all our thoughts and actions come together. These are our steady convictions. If our karma does not bring us back to the steady set of values, the music of karma in our lives will be more noise than music. That is the reason our wise ones always brought us back to the four eternal goals.

Comfort and Convenience

It is always tempting to stay within our comfort zone. But life is often not that convenient. Our convictions might be outside. Sticking to our beliefs might not only be difficult but also cause short-term losses. The biggest advantage in steady convictions is the lack of mental stress. Internal steadiness will help us withstand storms that we are bound to face in our lives.

Yet, what exactly defines our comfort zone? Does comfort equate security? These questions are best answered by taking a very careful look at what our convictions are, if any. Are these a set of beliefs defined by external sources or are these beliefs based on eternal knowledge and experience? The problem with living by a set of externally defined beliefs is that they are not truly convictions that can stand the test of obstacles and difficulties. They only provide the convenience of not having to explain our thoughts and actions to those around us. The problem with this approach is that the people around us do not have the capacity to protect us.

Prahlada

The concept of conviction and its underlying strength is best understood by looking at the character of a little boy named Prahlada in the Srimad Bhagavata Purana. This story not only portrays an amazing character but demonstrates the amazing strength of conviction and its role in the path to success.

Let us look at the cast of characters in this story. Kashyap is a divine sage or rishi. He has two wives, Diti and Aditi. The clan that resulted from the union of Kashyap and Diti is called Ditya, and the clan that resulted from the union of Kashyap and Aditi is called Aditya. While the Aditya clan produced divine beings, the Ditya clan produced demonic beings. The foremost among the Ditya clan are the two infamous brothers Hiranyaksha and Hiranyakashipu.

Many a time, when we are told about divine and demonic forces or beings, we brush it off as superstitious nonsense. But these entities can actually influence our thoughts and actions. For instance, the names Hiranyaksha and Hiranyakashipu mean 'one who has eyes set on wealth' and 'one who hides his wealth', respectively. Surely, we can feel their influence in present-day society.

In this demonic clan, a gem was born. His name was Prahlada. His father was Hiranyakashipu, a powerful king who was intoxicated with his wealth and power. He did not like the idea of the presence of a God (Lord Vishnu) who was more powerful. So, he set out to do something about it. At that time, Hiranyakashipu's queen, Kayadu, was pregnant with Prahlada. So, Hiranyakashipu took the pregnant Kayadu to a monastery in the forest and proceeded to perform austere penance dedicated to Chaturmukha Brahma, who had control over the entire material universe. Pleased with Hiranyakashipu, Lord Brahma appeared and asked what Hiranyakashipu wanted. Hiranyakashipu asked for a boon, which was granted by Brahma. The boon prevented Hiranyakashipu from being killed by either man or animal, either inside or outside his palace and either during the day or night. Armed with this boon, Hiranyakashipu thought he was invincible and started a reign of terror.

In the meantime, the seeds of his destruction had already been sown. While Hiranyakashipu was performing penance, the celestial sage Narada appeared to Kayadu and instructed her about the ultimate power of Lord Vishnu. Even though this had little effect on Kayadu, it was absorbed by Prahlada in his mother's womb. The ultimate power of Vishnu became a conviction for Prahlada, which stayed with him for an entire life and beyond.

Narasimha

As Prahlad started growing from a baby to a toddler, Hiranyakashipu was suffering from a dilemma—at times, he felt all-powerful, but, at other times, he would be afraid of somehow being destroyed by Lord Vishnu. So, he made sure that all theistic and spiritual material was removed from his kingdom. He instructed Prahlada's teachers to make sure that there was no mention of God in his instructions. But all of this was futile, as Prahlada had already formed rock-solid convictions.

Hiranyakashipu was horrified and confused by his toddler son's unshakable devotion towards Lord Vishnu. He tried gentle persuasion, threats and even excessive punishment to change his son's firm beliefs, but to no avail. This led Hiranyakashipu to immense anger and uncontrollable rage. He asked his son where he got the power to be so steadfast in his convictions. Prahlada told his father that he got it from God, from where Hiranyakashipu also got his power. Prahlada went on to say that God was all-pervasive and omnipotent.

Completely frustrated, Hiranyakashipu asked Prahlada if God was present in a pillar that they were standing near. Prahlada said that it was absolutely correct. At this, Hiranyakashipu kicked the pillar out of frustration. Just then, a strange form, half-lion and half-human, materialized from the pillar. This avatar of Vishnu is called Narasimha, the man-lion. It seized Hiranyakashipu and dragged him to the threshold of the palace entrance. The time was dusk, neither day nor night. That was the end of Hiranyakashipu. Prahlada was throned as the king and theism was brough back to the world.

Lessons Learnt

The very first point to be noticed is the fact that Prahlada received his instruction from Narada even before he was born. The problem with us is that we find it difficult to accept the truth as we grow up. We use our intelligence to argue against what we intuitively know to be the truth. So, to have proper beliefs and convictions, we need to look at the world with childlike innocence. That is easy to say but hard to implement.

The second point to be noticed is the ability of Prahlada to face difficulty (in this case, his father's threats). Firm convictions have the ability to imbue in us enormous mental strength in the face of adversity. Mental strength is far more powerful than physical strength.

The third lesson is that we are never alone in facing difficulty. There is a Universal Intelligence that is invisible and yet omnipresent. The question is not whether it is present but whether we feel its presence.

The story also proves the futility of using one's shrewdness and intelligence to outsmart the Infinite. Hiranyakashipu thought that he was safe since he had covered all possibilities of danger when he asked for the boon from Brahma. But the very fact that he performed austere penance shows that he was aware of bigger forces in the universe. Yet, he was foolish enough to think that he could outsmart them, resulting in tragic consequences.

But the most important lesson is the relationship between Prahlada's conviction, his firm stand in overcoming difficulties and his eventual success. This approach to success is neither easy nor convenient. But it affords one a sense of fearlessness, based on the knowledge that the path is a righteous one.

YOGA

Yoga is a universal concept. However, the yoga we understand to some extent and practise is the yogasana aspect. Even though this is useful and has a lot of positive impact on both physical and mental health, the concept of yoga is much deeper and holistic. It has an impact not only on the body and mind but also on the spirit.

At a foundational level, yoga is about balance. All the traits that we have discussed in the previous chapters have led to a balance of the mind, intellect and the spirit. This balance is needed for stability, particularly in times of difficulties. Just like constant falls can cause injuries, failures on the path to achieving a goal can be both painful and detrimental to success.

Duality is a part of nature. The two opposing sides actually hold the valuable part between them, just as the two sides that make up a coin, which is valuable as a whole. This duality and the best way to deal with it form the basis of the Bhagavad Gita. This text is an eternal guide to mastery over the senses, mind and intellect. It talks about the best way to accomplish success without the fear of failure.

Victory and Defeat

In verse 38, chapter 2 of the Bhagavad Gita, Shri Krishna tells Arjuna that if one were to view comfort and distress, profit and loss, victory and defeat equally, then no negative karma is accrued while engaging in a just fight. It is worth contemplating on this lesson.

In the first place, why should I not rejoice in victory? What is wrong in being excited about my success? Don't I deserve a pat on the back for a job well done? Furthermore, how can I be uncaring about defeat? Can I just say 'Oh, well' and move on? Would I do that if I really cared about the results?

All of these are equally valid questions. The teachings of Shri Krishna do not say one should not rejoice in victory. What should be avoided is looking at victory or defeat as 'my victory' or 'my defeat'. After all, if we could control the outcome, we would always opt for victory. When one tries to take all credit, intoxication will follow victory, and depression will follow defeat. If we were to look at victory and defeat as a part of a bigger plan managed by an unseen higher power, both intoxication and depression can be avoided.

As in case of profit and loss, the two sides of engaging in any business, it would be possible to deal with both on an equal footing if the purpose of engaging in business is not mere increasing personal wealth for personal enjoyment. After keeping a fair amount as personal gain, if the excess wealth is distributed among the deserving in society, there will be no sense of ownership of the acquired wealth.

As far as comfort and difficulties are concerned, our actual needs are fairly minimal. The problem arises when we mistake our wants for needs. In such a scenario, our needs are not what is essential for a comfortable life but represent our insatiable greed. Thus, it would be impossible to maintain balance, mentally and spiritually, if satisfaction is based on a moving target.

If we were to actually follow the teaching in this lesson, our thought, speech and action should be one of gratitude towards the one who is in the driver's seat, i.e. God. Then we can accept any outcome without overexcitement or extreme anguish. Since the outcome is for the broader good and not personal gain, no bad karma will be accrued.

Action and Reaction

In the same chapter of the Bhagavad Gita, Shri Krishna expands on karma and its rewards in verse 47. He says every person has the right to perform karma but not its rewards. He says that we should neither consider ourselves to be the cause of fruits of labour nor indulge in inaction.

This can be a little confusing. Why would anyone perform karma with enthusiasm if they cannot expect results of the karma? Will this not lead to inaction eventually? These confusions arise when we think that we should not have expectations. The message says that we should not make the fruits of labour a prerequisite for performing the labour. One reason for this advice is that a focus on the outcome and its implications could make us lose focus on the labour itself. This would naturally result in subpar results.

So, why should we not consider ourselves to be the cause of our karma? Again, it is not that we are not the cause but that we are not the only cause. We may be the cause of intent and effort. But we are not born with the knowledge of performing the karma. One or more teachers teach us many things, over time, that culminate in our karma. They, too, deserve credit for the knowledge that made the action possible. Lastly, so many things in the universe have to come together for anything to happen. Only God can make all of these things come together. So, he deserves the most credit for any karma. This knowledge enables us to focus on the job at hand and not on its outcome.

Inaction is never an option in life. Like a wheel in motion, life keeps moving in the right direction. When we indulge in action, for whatever reason, we are likely to lose our balance and fall, figuratively speaking. But every successful person understands this concept and maintains balance through victory and defeat. The outcome, desirable or not, will never deter him or her from sincere effort. Any defeat only becomes a source of learning worthy of analysis. It is the lesson learnt in defeat that increases the probability of victory in subsequent attempts.

Stability

Again, in chapter 2 of the Bhagavad Gita, Arjuna asks Shri Krishna as to what a person with stillness and stability looks like. How does he sit, stand and speak? Even though Shri Krishna does not directly answer the question, he only describes the traits of such a person.

The cravings of the senses naturally upset the mind. The mind starts wandering and gets fixated on prior sensory pleasures. What starts off as a desire for sensory pleasure gradually turns into obsession and craving. So, a steadfast person will try to consciously cut off the cravings of the senses. He or she will be satisfied with whatever comes his way in terms of selfish pleasures. The mind is trainable. So, after some time, it will start obsessing over sensory pleasures. It does not mean that we should not enjoy sensory pleasures. Mental stability is not upset by enjoyment but rather by craving and obsession.

Our acquisitions can also create an unsteady mind. We may see or hear about something that appears to be attractive. We may go after it with a passion. There are only two possible outcomes. If we happen to get it, we may start to form an attachment to the object, which would lead to fear of losing it. If, on the other hand, we are unable to acquire it, we become angry. Both of these emotions, anger and fear, will only cause instability and make us lose our mental balance.

Tortoise and the Shell

In verse 58 of chapter 2 of the Bhagavad Gita, Shri Krishna gives a wonderful analogy to explain how a person with a steadfast balance operates. He uses the analogy of a tortoise. The moment it senses danger, it quickly withdraws all its limbs and head into the shell. Similarly, a steadfast person will withdraw all his senses when he perceives danger.

This analogy offers more than what appears on the surface. The tortoise normally lives in water. Its limbs are designed for smooth swimming in water. But it occasionally comes out of the water to enjoy direct sunlight on land. It moves slowly and somewhat awkwardly on land. It is also more susceptible to danger on land.

We are also similar. A person who is immersed in sensory pleasures is like a fish swimming in water. We will be immersed in the universe and not even realize that there is a world beyond. A fish is constantly drinking water and gets whatever little oxygen from the water. We, too, constantly consume the pleasures of the universe and get whatever little spiritual energy that we can from our surroundings.

We normally can never see what is beyond.

But through constant effort, like a tortoise, we can develop a shell of protection called jnana or wisdom. When we have acquired this jnana, we, too, can escape sensory pleasures and briefly step outside to absorb the energy that is present outside the universe of sensory pleasures. While we may be somewhat awkward in these unnatural surroundings, we will have the ability to withdraw our senses and the mind under the protective shell of wisdom.

Danger of Destruction

Perhaps the best lesson on avoiding the danger of destruction is verse 62 and 63 of chapter 2 of the Bhagavad Gita. The problem always starts with contemplation of the objects of sensory pleasure. With constant thought of these pleasures, one develops an attachment to the objects of pleasure. These attachments lead to desire and the pursuit of these objects. The chances of not getting our desires satisfied are high. That almost always leads to anger.

We know that we do not think straight when we are angry. We get confused and act irrational. That leads to loss of memory. We forget lessons learnt from the past. The intellect relies heavily on memory. So, when we lose our memory, our intellect is destroyed. When the intellect is destroyed, all is lost.

So, to maintain balance, a successful person builds upon all the strengths gained from the seven traits that we have discussed so far. But to avoid destruction and losing everything, one has to constantly watch out for losing balance by maintaining a firm control over the pursuit of sensory pleasures.

PRANA SHAKTI

Movement is life. Every living object is in constant motion and change. When all change and motion ceases, we say that a person has become lifeless. Whether it is physical, mental or spiritual, change and motion needs energy. This life-giving and life-sustaining energy is what is called 'prana shakti'.

Matter and energy are the two aspects of the universe. The entire universe is an interplay of these two aspects. While both aspects are important, energy plays a more important role. While a not-so-perfect body can function fairly well with good *pranic* (life-sustaining) energy, a perfect physical body is useless without the life-sustaining energy.

In Vedic tradition, more importance was given to energy than the material side of things. Every karma was turned into a spiritual exercise to ensure that good energy propelled it towards a successful outcome. The western thought process is more inclined towards the material outcome.

The Energy Layer

The human body is called *sadhana shareera* in Sanskrit. It is different from all other species of animal life. Man can do things that are out of proportion to his physical attributes. What gives man this enormous skill is the manner in which the different layers are structured.

According to Vedic texts, the sadhana shareera is made up of five layers. Each layer is called a *kosha*. The outermost layer is the *annamaya kosha*, which is the physical body. Even though we tend to pay an undeserving amount of attention to the physical self, the underlying layers have an enormous impact on the well-being of the physical body.

The third layer is the mental layer. This is the layer that is involved in the creation and manipulation of all thoughts that control all the actions of the physical body. Not to be confused with the brain; the mind and the intellect are not physical. This is similar to the way the modern computer works. While the brain is like the processor in the hardware, the mind and the intellect are like the software that drives the actions of the hardware. This layer is the *manomaya kosha*.

Nestled between the annamaya kosha and the manomaya kosha, the second layer, is the energy layer called *pranamaya kosha*. This layer is what drives the activity and preserves the well-being of both the physical and mental layers. It is also the interface between the body and the mind. As such, it is extremely important that we pay close attention to a healthy energy layer. Almost all Vedic spiritual activities involve the exercise of pranayama. Unfortunately, this has been misunderstood to be a breathing exercise. Mere breathing exercises, while being beneficial for the body, cannot impact the energy layer. Performing pranayama on a regular basis requires proper instruction and training, under a proper guru.

The energy of a person manifests itself through several observable characteristics. Positive prana shakti is a trait observable in all successful people. They never seem to get tired, both physically and mentally. They seem to have enormous stamina to keep going, even under difficult circumstances. They seem to have a very sharp intellect, capable of quick and correct decision-making. They can overcome physical ailments in a short span.

The last two layers are the *vijnanamaya kosha* and the *anandamaya kosha*. Chitta is another name for vijnanamaya kosha and is a permanent memory shell that stays with us through every cycle of birth and death. It provides a continuity to the jiva, or soul, through the cycle of rebirth. Anandamaya kosha is the actual jiva in its original form of jnana and *ananda* (bliss).

Energy and the Environment

While it is essential to create positive energy within ourselves, it is equally important to create positive energy in our surroundings. While our prana shakti mostly impacts ourselves, the presence of positive energy in our surroundings affects society at large. Keeping this in mind, Vedic tradition expected us to perform karma specifically aimed at cleansing our environment for the good of all.

It is with this goal in mind that the Vedic karma of *homa* was designed. While there are many variations of homa, with different results expected, it serves the common purpose of creating positive energy in society. It is unfortunate that this karma has morphed into a personal and commercial activity.

To start with, it is not an exercise in making sacrificial offerings through fire. A fire is a material object that can burn only the things put in it. It does not have the ability to do anything by itself. However, the divine entity that controls all forms of elevated energy is Agni, and fire is merely a physical manifestation of this divine force. In Sanskrit, the etymology of the word 'Agni' gives an indication of this divine entity. Agni can be split as a+ga+ni. The consonant ga means 'to go' or 'to move'; a+ga means 'something that cannot move' or 'something inert'; a+ga+ni means 'something that can give movement to the inert'. It is the energy needed for movement.

So, we can create positive energy by offering the right thought and material to Agni, the divine entity. The most important substance that is offered is ghee. Again, it is not merely the physical substance but the thought that it represents that makes a difference in our surroundings.

In Vedic tradition, the cow represents 'Veda Mata' or the 'mother of all knowledge'. Milk from this divine mother is representative of Vedic knowledge. So, we can acquire all the Vedic knowledge but cannot offer it back directly, just as we cannot offer milk directly in fire.

This knowledge has to be taken to higher energy levels by meditation. This is similar to the milk being boiled and cooled. When we add a few drops of curd or yogurt to the boiled milk, it solidifies into yogurt. Similarly, the *upadesha* or initiation by a true guru will solidify our knowledge.

When we churn yogurt, butter is formed magically after some time. Similarly, when we constantly apply the solidified knowledge we have acquired, true bhakti (as explained in Chapter 2) will emanate. But even this has *rajasik* and *tamasik* components, which are horizontal and downward moving components.

When we boil butter and strain it, we end up with pure ghee. Similarly, when we seriously examine our bhakti and put it to test, we can recognize and remove all unwanted components in it. It is this clarified and purified bhakti that we offer to Agni during homa.

Another component that is essential for homa is the mantra. This will dictate where the offerings are directed and what the specific results will be. But irrespective of type of homa that is performed, the common goal is to create positive energy in our surroundings. This will ensure that negative energies are removed. Once we are in a clean spiritual environment, only then can we focus on good karma, both for ourselves and society at large.

Energy and Hanuman

In the Ramayana, the character of Hanuman stands out when we think of what strength and energy can accomplish. He is the very personification of seemingly limitless energy. The prana shakti of Hanuman manifests in many forms in the face of adversity.

The very first incident is when he volunteers to jump over the sea to Lanka to find Sita. When he is standing on the seashore looking towards Lanka, other monkeys come and ask if he is afraid and has doubts about his ability to accomplish the given task. He replies that he is like an arrow shot from the bow of Sri Ram. It will not only go far enough but shall never miss the target. The confidence in his ability, without being arrogant, is the nature of the one who is bestowed with real strength.

Another incident worth mentioning occured during his flight to Lanka. A demoness called Simhika challenges him. She says that Hanuman has to enter her mouth. He becomes small, enters her mouth and grows large inside her, destroying her as a consequence. These stories should not be taken literally. It signifies the ability of a person endowed with enormous energy to operate at any level of strength. Such a person can alter his stature, mentally and spiritually, to suit any context. This enables him to deal with both small and large difficulties on an equal footing.

In the court of King Ravana, Hanuman's tail is set on fire to teach him a lesson. But Hanuman, with boundless energy, jumps from rooftop to rooftop, setting the entire city of Lanka on fire, before extinguishing the fire in the ocean. It shows how his energy totally reverses the fortunes of those who try to harm him.

In another situation, Laxman is badly injured by Indrajit, the son of King Ravana. Hanuman is tasked with sourcing the herb *sanjeevani* from the mountain Dronagiri. Upon reaching the mountain and unable to recognize the herb, he lifts the entire mountain and brings it to the battlefield. Laxman is thus saved from the debilitating injury.

The Lesson

One could look at all these stories and conclude that they are too fantastical to be real or are not of any use. But if one looks beyond the superficial, there are some very important lessons on the role of prana shakti or the energy layer in each of us.

Developing positive energy can give us the ability to take quick and intelligent decisions, resulting in decisive actions. Fearlessness comes to the one who has the energy to accomplish even seemingly impossible tasks.

It is this energy that can cure us of ailments, both physical and mental. This is a broad solution to a myriad of ailments that can afflict us. Even when we are unable to diagnose a specific ailment or identify its cure, good prana shakti can ensure overall good health.

And inevitably, the energy will manifest as strength. Even the worst and most powerful of our enemies cannot harm us. When they try, their misdeeds will only backfire and result in their own destruction. It helps us stay focused, be constantly aware of the obstacles and eventually leads us to success in attaining our goals.

BALA

'**B**ala', or strength, leads to success. It is not mere physical strength or even mental strength. It is the strength of the universe that gets channelled through us, as part of a much bigger agenda. This requires both alignment with a bigger purpose and being constantly connected to the flow of energy.

All the nine traits that we have examined so far automatically lead to the ultimate trait, bala, which is the strength needed to reach any goal. The important factor to consider is whether success in a given pursuit will only benefit us or have a positive impact on a larger group of people in society.

Starting with the pursuit of correct and resourceful knowledge, following and developing all the 10 traits is a gradual process. It is also a lifelong process. It is a parallel process in which we observe a steady progress and growth in all the traits, in many directions. These could include personal growth, professional growth and even spiritual growth. After all, they are all connected, and this wheel of success is what will take us far in a given lifetime.

Intellectual Strength

Not to be confused with intelligence in processing information, intellectual strength is the foundation on which our values are built. A strong set of values will help us stay on track, in spite of distractions along the way. It will also help us avoid the danger of short-term benefits derailing the journey towards long-term benefits.

It is not uncommon to find that personal values,

sometimes, are orthogonal to societal values. Often societal values are dictated by personal agenda of the rich and powerful. However, our personal intellectual strength can help us navigate through these tricky situations.

Intellectual strength also helps us in understanding and appreciating the way of life that our ancestors followed. These eternal set of values are permanent in *sanatana dharma*, the value system on which the Vedic way of life is based. It is a system that is always upward-looking, in harmony with nature and spiritually uplifting. It is a system that fills the journey of life with bliss. It is a life that gets rid of all negative energy.

Physical and Mental Strength

Life is a marathon and not a sprint. It needs stamina, both physical and mental. Sudden spurts of energy do not ensure successful outcomes. The strength needed is not a mere outcome of healthy eating and exercise. The human system is a holistic one. Strengthening the parts does not necessarily strengthen the whole.

Naturally, we need a healthy and strong physical body. This is not mere muscle power. We need to have a strong immune system that is capable of fighting disease. Even when we are infected, the body should have the strength to bounce back quickly. Developing healthy habits and living a life of virtue will ensure all of these.

Even though it is often ignored, good mental health is as important as or perhaps even more important than physical strength. Many of the traits that have been discussed before aid the achievement of optimal mental balance and strength. Mental disease is harder to diagnose and treat. It can manifest in many forms, resulting in negative outcomes such as anger, jealousy and depression. Developing these traits can definitely overcome many of these problems.

Victory

All of us aspire for victory. This may involve a situation of competition with others. Or it might be just reaching a desired goal. Failures, often touted as stepping stones to success, are not really something we look forward to. Even though we can definitely learn our lessons from mistakes and failures, it is more desirable to learn the lessons to avoid failures.

A methodical approach towards success, as outlined in this book, can lead to positive outcomes every time. Success breeds more success. Every victory makes us more confident in our abilities. It gives us more faith in the righteousness of the universe and its creator. It turns our faith into experiences. These positive experiences help us turn our knowledge into wisdom.

This wisdom, again, becomes the starting point that leads to passion, which, in turn, drives other initiatives. The circle of successful outcomes will take us far in life. More than any selfish motive, we become the symbol of strength that others can lean on. We become the pillars of strength that remain standing when the storms have passed.

Courage

If there is one thing that we should all aspire for, it is courage. When we have the conviction and experience that we will always be protected, we will always be courageous. Very often, people know that their motives may not be all that noble. Even if they swear to the contrary, they might be aware that they are doing something wrong. Such people can never be courageous.

On the other hand, if we know that we are on the path of dharma, we can always be sure that we will be protected. Even though it would be foolish to be not cautious, we can take calculated risks for high returns. This would be analogous to climbing a mountain. There is always the risk of falling, but that does not stop a courageous climber from aiming for the peak.

So, this, too, is a type of inner strength. It helps us move forward with confidence, even if there are chances of failure. It allows us to step out of our comfort zones. It is the courage to venture into uncharted waters that can help us discover unknown lands. It is indeed a necessary trait in anyone who seeks success in life.

Lack of Fear

Fear comes from darkness. This is not mere absence of light. It is the inner darkness that plunges us into the depths of negative energy. Sometimes, we fear people who appear to be more powerful than us. Sometimes, we fear situations that appear to spin out of control. We feel helpless.

But a person with inner strength has no fear. Because his strength is based on knowledge. This knowledge, if upward-oriented, will remove all fear and darkness within. He will be aware that even people who appear to be very strong derive their strength from the Infinite. Nothing happens in an independent fashion. Nobody can hurt us unless our karma dictates that we should be hurt.

Situations are never out of control. The fact is that we never have control over any situation. We just labour under the illusion that we have control. This is the basic teaching of the Bhagavad Gita. When we hand over the reins to Shri Krishna, we can focus on the task at hand and become successful. Since we cannot fathom destiny, we might as well leave the workings of destiny in the hands of the one who controls it. His strength will be our strength.

Free from Disease

As evident in the last two years, disease can create worldwide panic and havoc. These diseases can be due to abnormalities within or infections from outside. We cannot completely avoid either of them. Internal abnormalities may be genetic, caused by normal wear and tear or due to bad lifestyle choices. External infections can be due to physical contact with others or even airborne and waterborne infections. Similar afflictions might ravage the mind as well.

Even though we may not be able to avoid contact with diseases, a strong person can fight them off with minimal long-term damage. The human body is an amazing system capable of both self-correction and adaptation. Both spiritual and mental strength and energy can effectively heal every physical ailment. Many a time, spiritual healing can eliminate diseases with no side effects.

So, real strength implies both immunity from external physical threats and adaptation to internal abnormalities. A guru, in Vedic tradition, is both a teacher and a healer. Those who have experienced it know that this truly gives us freedom from disease.

Lethargy

Every productive and successful person has this one noticeable trait—lack of lethargy. An inability to overcome lethargy can turn even the most capable person into an unproductive and useless person. Lethargy is a weakness, sometimes physical and sometimes mental.

We get tired of doing something only when it is a chore. If it is an act of love, we never get tired of it. We do not get tired from it either. On the contrary, it energizes us and is a source of motivation to do more. So, the trick is to align our thoughts, actions and speech with something that we are truly passionate about.

A truly passionate person will have other traits such as belief in the value of the desired outcome, confidence in the process and conviction in the greater good. Productivity is a strength that can keep us on track, even when the task is physically or mentally strenuous. When the job is completed, even the hardships leave only a pleasant tiredness. That is the only way to rest before embarking on the next task.

Eloquence

Our ability to eloquently translate our thoughts into speech is important when interacting and communicating with the external world. We should not be searching for words or stumbling when we speak. A seamless flow of thought to speech is indeed one of the strengths of a successful person.

When thoughts themselves are not clear, it would be impossible for speech to be clear. Clarity of thought comes from many of the traits that have been discussed before. These thoughts cannot be clouded with doubts about our goals or about the path taken to reach the goal.

Sometimes, our thoughts are clear. But we may be unable to convey them in words. This is because our communication is not a mere collection of words but the energy contained in the silence between the words. This energy can also manifest in body language and the look in our eyes. The energy contained in our speech is quite clear to the listener. The strength of our words depends on the inner strength that drives the speech.

EPILOGUE

We have discussed 10 traits in this book, starting from knowledge and ending with strength in its many forms. This is the path that I adopted in my own personal pursuit of success. It has not only resulted in professional success but also taken me farther than I expected in my personal and spiritual journey of life.

It has filled my life with optimism and excitement. It has helped me envision tasks that seemed too big at the start. It has also helped me engage with hundreds of people who aligned themselves with my cause. It has continuously brought amazing people into my life. It has given me an opportunity to experience things that I was not even aware of.

More than anything else, this journey has brought me tremendous bliss. This bliss has dwarfed all obstacles and difficulties. Even today, it makes me wake up every morning with excitement and go to sleep with the satisfaction of a job well done.

ACKNOWLEDGEMENTS

My gratitude to my guru, the late Dr Bannanje Govindacharya, is beyond words. He totally changed the direction of my life by awakening the thirst for spiritual knowledge in me. His affection and compassion towards me were beyond my worth. All the thoughts expressed in this book came directly or indirectly from him.

Many wonderful people have accompanied me as fellow travellers through life. Teachers, students and friends have all contributed to my education about life. In particular, I have to thank my wife Dr Vanditha Mukund, my daughters Kavitha and Anupama, my sons-in-law Pramod and Dhruva, and my grandchildren Praveer, Kaveri, Tara and

Kabini. They make sure that there is never a dull moment in my life.

My thanks to Rupa Publications for publishing this book. In particular, the enthusiasm and excitement of Dibakar Ghosh was very touching and encouraging. The meticulous editing by Upama Biswas has made this a much better book. My thanks to both of them.

Lastly, my eternal gratitude to my adi guru Shri Madhvacharya and the Supreme Lord Shri Krishna for accepting me as their servant.